He loves him: Gay story

By Susan R. Garza

Table of content

Chapter 1

Frank's point of view

When my door opened to show a very happy Kelvin, I was reading a book in my room. He was beaming like a lotto winner. He walked up to me and gave me a hard embrace. I hope that this moment won't last, but when my lungs begin to stop taking a breath, I'm out of luck.

I am unable to breathe. I remarked as he let go of that vicious embrace.

"Sorry." He said "sorry,"

"What makes you so joyful? Did you win the lotto, if so, how?" I smiled at him and inquired.

I'll tell you what. While resting his hands on my shoulder, he spoke to me.

"I already had a good idea long ago," I remarked in a mocking tone.

"Finally, she gave her approval! Woooohh! I own Nelly Parker!" He remarked while lifting both of his hands.

I heard something crack, but was it a glass or a heart?

There were no broken glasses everywhere that I looked. I was correct. My heart was shattered by it. broken into numerous pieces like glass that was hurled against a wall.

I just said "Oh."

How miserable I am.

I felt a tear start to roll down my face as I stared down at the ground.

He stopped applauding and turned to face me.

"Are you alright?" He queried. I just nodded in response.

"What's wrong with you? " He asked once again as he dried my tears.

"tears of delight I just rejoice for you," I said, grinning comfortingly at him.

A grin that would hide my dejected demeanor.

He is unaware of my affection for him.

Frank, you're such a moron. As straight as a pole, he wouldn't adore you the way you do.

My mind informed me.

I am aware that it might be dangerous to fall in love with a straight man, particularly if he is also your closest friend.

His pocket-containing phone rang. He pulled it out and responded to the caller.

"Hello, my name is Kelvin... I'm with Frank here. Baby, I'll be there. Bye." As he said, he slid his phone back into his pocket.

"I should go right now. Today, I'm heading to her home. Must go." I was left alone in my room as he hurried out the door.

I am handed the book I was reading. The book is covered with drips of wetness. I lost the ability to grasp what I was reading.

I thus shut it and set it on the table.

I sit down on my bed and start crying nonstop.

I'm a moron.

Kelvin's point of view

I've been dating Nelly for two months. We've been spending all of our time together in my room. every Saturday and Sunday after school. We were always together.

I remain at her side in school as well. I was never able to spend time with my best buddy.

Concerning that, ever since I informed him about Nelly, he has been behaving strangely. He had never stopped working. He no longer frequents the cafeteria since he is always reading at the library. He continues to read as he is going to his residence.

I suppose I ought to invite him to join me this Friday. Yes, that should be a wise decision. I'll ask my colleagues as well.

I'm now attempting to sleep while resting on my bed.

The verb to use is "trying."

Tonight, Nelly is here with me. She requested permission to spend the night since it was pouring so heavily. She is now speaking about her day.

Although I truly want to sleep, I must pay attention to her. She shouldn't despise me, I hope.

She eventually slept out next to me. I then lay down on the bed and let myself be consumed by the darkness.

Time skipped to Friday.

Hello, Frank. I asked him to come. From the book he was reading, he raised his head.

"What?" He started with a serious expression. He's been acting solemnly recently.

"Would you want to join me and my pals for some fun?" I quizzed him. In response, he just nodded before continuing his walk.

After that, I went to my first period.

Dull classes continued when the school bell sounded.

Thank God for lunch.

I went to where we usually sit in the cafeteria. Next to me was my girlfriend.

Hey, have you heard the news that's been going around? Darby suddenly questioned.

"No," I said.

"Who are you as a best friend? The previous book was being read by Frank at the library. He finished reading every book in the library." He spoke.

"The librarian requested Frank and informed the principal about it. He was forced to take a test. the examination that college graduates have to take. They said he understood everything well, and when they asked him whether he wanted to enroll in college, he declined for an unknown reason." He spoke.

Wow, such a brilliant guy.

Why didn't he tell me, I wonder.

Timing skip

Outside, it was drizzling heavily. We were watching "Fifty Shades of Grey" while seated in the living room.

To be honest, including myself, the males around here have difficulties covering the bulges in their trousers. Damn, there are so many sex scenes in this movie.

The doorbell rang abruptly. I want to open it and show a wet Frank inside.

I questioned, "Why were you so wet?

"I was walking here when it started pouring rain." He wrung his shirt as he reacted.

"Come take off your clothes and get in the shower," I said.

He moved away from me and toward my room.

I responded, bringing him the towel, "Here."

You are welcome to some of my clothing. I continued, and he immediately went to the restroom. After leaving my room, I returned to the main room.

After a little while, my door to the room opened to see...

Holy crap!

Chapter 2

Frank's point of view

I was digging around in his dresser for items that could fit. He wore large shorts.

My black tight boxer from the day we had a sleepover is the only item I discovered after digging through his drawers for a while.

I left the room to see if he had any clothing that would suit me.

"Okay, Kelvin? Can you just come here for a moment?" I remarked as I was alone with a boxer outside the room.

I saw that he was slightly opening his lips while he was staring at me. His expression was one of total amazement. Nelly was the only other man doing the same thing as I turned to look around.

She glared at me.

They turned aside as I uncomfortably cleared my throat. Every time Kelvin invited us to hang out with him, they invariably saw me without a shirt.

"What?" questioned Kelvin.

"Uh, I need a little assistance here," I said clumsily.

When I went inside the room, he followed.

"What do you need support for?" He inquired while attempting to avert my gaze by glancing elsewhere.

"Can I borrow some of your clothing for the evening? I refer to clothing that would suit me." While rubbing the back of my neck, I questioned him.

"Oh. Yeah. You left some clothing behind." He walked over to a neighboring drawer and took some clothing out.

"Here. Your long-sleeved top and your sleeveless shirt." He displayed the two shirts to me.

It's chilly, so I chose the long-sleeved one. It extends beyond my thighs and covers my boxer.

I'm sorry, but I don't have any shorts that fit you. He rubbed his neck while grinning. He gave me a direct glance. glaring at one another.

We stood there for a minute. My heart is beating a lot faster. Although he already loves someone, I truly do adore him. That hurts so badly because I adore him.

I averted my eyes and said, "Thanks," before turning to go.

When a sudden event prevented me from opening the door, I was just about to.

Kelvin's point of view

Who knows how long we exchanged eye contact? His eyes were so full of feelings.

Later, he turned his gaze away. His expression was dejected.

But I stopped him before he could open the door.

I gave him a deep embrace and drew him to my chest.

"I am aware that there is a problem. Inform me." I informed him. He has a problem because I can see it in his eyes.

He released the embrace and fixed his eyes on mine.

"Nothing is incorrect. I'm good." He murmured, giving me a comforting grin. He's lying but I let it go for now. I'll have to question him one day.

Both of us leave the room. Darby has been glancing at him strangely, I've observed.

Returning to my position between Darby and Nelly, I got up.

Frank sat backward from the group and crossed his legs in front of him. He may not have read any books, which surprises me. the absence of a book at this location. I chuckled to myself at my dimwitted mentality.

We kept on watching the film until someone gently elbowed me to get my attention. I cocked an eyebrow at Darby as I turned to gaze to my right.

Can I ask you a question? He spoke in a low voice.

"Yeah. It is what?" I remarked, being more interested in what it is.

"Could we first go someplace private? And if I told you, please don't panic. Deal?" He spoke.

"Deal. Let's now go to the backyard." I said as I again excused myself and left the room for the lawn.

He was slightly trembling when we got to the backyard. He feels anxious.

God alone knows how long we stood there until I broke the awkward quiet.

"So, guy, what is it?" I queried, feeling a little irritated.

I was astonished by the question he asked.

WHAT THE FUCK!!!

Chapter 3

Kelvin's point of view

"I'm carrying your kid," I said. He remarked while lowering his gaze.

Widening, I stared at him in disbelief. The atmosphere was silent.

HOW DARE YOU!

Later, I overheard him laughing.

I questioned him, "Why are you laughing?"

"Dude, I didn't have sex with you, and men cannot become pregnant. You ought to have noticed your face." After another chuckle, he said.

How foolish am I? Naturally, I avoided having sex with him. I gave him a shoulder punch that caused him to stumble.

I began to leave since I'm so furious with him. He stopped me before I could get to the door.

"Wait! I must discuss Frank with you right now. Ok, I'm sorry." He remarked, releasing his hold on my hand.

What happened to him? I inquired, sounding irate.

"Can I, well, date him because you're his closest friend?" He queried.

Wow, I see why he's been behaving strangely now.

"Um, yeah, you can," I said. I said.

But only if you guarantee me not to harm him. Added I

"Okay. I swear. Regards, buddy." As he said, a guy hugged me.

As we got back inside, the movie had just concluded. I saw everyone stretching and yawning.

"I'm sleepy and worn out," Nelly said as she got to her feet and approached me.

"Sleep with me, baby." She said while kissing my lips.

Good night, fellas. I informed them. They just said, "Night," and then they fell asleep.

Nelly led me to my room, where she shut the door. She began kissing me, but I refrained from returning the favor.

"I'm sorry, but I'm worn out. Can we simply go to bed?" I murmured as I moved toward my bed.

"All well, but please make it up to me." I didn't respond to her, simply slackly lifted my thumb in response.

She joined me in bed after that.

noon

Frank's point of view

I moaned.

I have trouble falling asleep. I've been seeing the rainfall from where I'm seated in the living room, close to the window. Everyone in the guest room was sound sleeping.

My heart feels as if it is being stabbed by a dagger when I see them kissing.

I'm such a moron. Why did I decide to come here at all? Oh yes, my best buddy has a girlfriend, and I'm crazily in love with her. Great.

I moaned.

unable to sleep I overheard someone say. The individual sat next to me.

I glanced at the individual. It's Darby, I see.

Frank's point of view

unable to sleep I overheard someone say. The individual sat next to me.

I glanced at the individual. It's Darby, I see.

"Yeah. I've been thinking a lot recently." I said.

"What are you contemplating? You seem bothered by it." As he stared at me, he questioned.

Things, I uttered.

He groaned.

I would want the rain to cease. He remarked as he turned to face the window.

"I hope it doesn't," I informed him.

"I like the rain. I'm at ease because of that." He simply laughed as I continued.

"You're unusual but I like weird things. Strange individuals are special." He spoke. It caused me to flush.

I gave him a grin.

At least, people other than Kelvin like my eccentricity. I laughed as I said.

I'm experiencing heavy eyelids. I shut my eyes and lean on his shoulder. He said "good night" to me. Then, all is lost.

My face was bathed in sunlight when morning arrived. My waist felt like it had an arm wrapped around it. I glanced at the individual.

Darby's here.

We passed out on the sofa, I realized. I must have been carried by him.

Darby awoke and began to move. He grinned at me as he slowly opened his eyes.

"Happy morning. Do you feel rested?" He spoke.

I just grinned and nodded in response to him.

Louder footsteps could be heard.

Good morning, sweethearts! said Jake. He is a buddy of Kelvin's.

Darby just tossed him a pillow and struck him in the face.

Darby commanded, "Shut up."

I got up from the sofa and went to the kitchen. He followed suit as well.

Everyone in the kitchen was looking at Darby and me when I arrived.

"Uh, are you guys all right?" I questioned clumsily.

Kelvin grinned at Darby and remarked, "I smell something fishy."

Because you're eating tuna, of course, you'll smell fishy, Kelvin. Darby rolled his eyes and replied mockingly.

Breakfast was quiet.

Soon after that...

"Hey fellas, are you up for a trip? This place is dull." Kelvin questioned us.

Except for me, everyone else simply nodded.

"I can't," I said. Everyone turned to face me.

Why Darby questioned.

"I am busy. I have to complete the book I checked out." I said.

"Would you kindly accompany us?" He begged.

Please, oh please, could you? he added.

I gave him a minute of my attention.

I replied in a monotone, "Fine."

"YES!" When he said that, he leaped.

I laughed at his antics. He's such a baby.

We all headed home after breakfast to get dressed before meeting at the mall.

I showered and then brushed my teeth.

I then decided to put on a red blouse and a pair of slim jeans.

We're in the mall right now. Darby is the only one remaining when I say "us." I'm not being critical. He's a nice person, but we're not close.

I've been perusing the books in the bookshop where we visited. The novel

"Paper Towns by John Green" caught my attention. I'm very excited to read this book. I was astonished when I saw the price. It's pricey.

Putting it back on the shelf, I sighed. That book is one I truly desire.

For us to meet them at McDonald's, Kelvin texted. Darby advised me to move on since he had work to do.

When I arrived, I noticed that they were seated.

Who is Darby? They inquired.

He claimed he had things to do, so, um. I answered.

Jake responded, "All right.

A waiter approached and requested our order. We all decided to have a McBurger and a McFloat.

Our orders came through shortly after. Darby also showed up. He had a bag in his hand.

Hey, pleased you arrived. Kelvin said as they shook hands.

He questioned, "Where did you go anyway?"

He said, "To the bookshop and Hot Topic."

What did you purchase, Kelvin, enquired?

Darby handed it to me after reaching inside the bag for something.

It had a paper covering on it.

I did, and it was...

OMG!

Chapter 4

Frank's point of view

Darby sat down next to me when he got there.

What did you purchase, Kelvin, enquired?

Darby handed it to me after reaching inside the bag for something.

It had a paper covering on it.

I gasped when I opened it.

OMG! It's John Green's "The Fault in Our Stars." I adore his writings.

Darby, thank you so much! I remarked as I gave him a firm embrace.

"I had a feeling you'd like it. The second book is too pricey for me to purchase. Given that you enjoy John Green, I decided to get it instead." He spoke uncomfortably and scratched his head afterward.

"It's OK. I adore it so much." I said.

"I'll take you on a casual date, you know. Deal? How about Friday night?" Added I

He grinned as he turned to face me.

Yes! The deal, he replied.

Kelvin asked me if we could come.

"No doubt. More is always better." I said.

After finishing our meal, we visited a park. I'm reading the book Darby handed me while he played football with Kelvin, Darby, Jake, and the other boys.

Nelly was nowhere to be seen, and I realized it, but I ignored it.

Mother Nature called a little while later. I HAVE TO GO!

I quickly released it in the restroom after that. I hear wailing on the side as I exit.

I moved toward the source of the noise. I was astounded by what I saw.

The unknown man and Nelly were kissing and dry humping each other.

I grabbed my phone and snapped a photo. I'm glad they didn't see me.

I got up and walked back to the bench where I had been sitting. Kelvin would have to find out on his own, so I opted against telling him to avoid ruining the day. despite my want to.

It was growing dark as the sun sank. So, we made our way home.

I immediately went to my room and lay down.

I moaned.

Such a day.

Frank's point of view

The weekend sped by. Currently, I was readying for my friendly date with Darby. I then placed my phone in my pocket and stepped outside. I was heading over to Kelvin's place. He decided that we should all meet at his place as it is a double date.

I saw Nelly coming out of the door as I got closer to his home. She went away while grinning disturbingly.

When I heard the door slam shut violently, I turned away. This is not a good idea. Only when Kelvin is angry does the sound occur.

When I entered, I discovered smashed vases. I told Darby we had to reschedule when I saw her. Oh my, this is a disaster.

I entered his room and saw the mess he had created. He was draped in his blanket and was laying on his bed. There is just one meaning to this. He was aware of their breakup.

I just returned the items to their proper locations. For the last several years, this has been my daily routine. Every time his heart was crushed, he would act out badly.

I went to sit on his bed after a little bit of tidying up in his room.

What occurred this time, then? I queried.

She fucked up and cheated! He yelled and attempted to toss the alarm clock. "Tried" is the operative word because I stopped him from doing it. He would toss anything close to him, I knew.

"You'll be OK. You will endure." I said. You're fortunate to still have the closest friend that won't abandon you under any circumstances. Added I

He just kept quiet. We haven't spoken for a while. I used my phone to check the time.

"Hey, I have to go. Time is running out." I said. I needed to use the restroom. But first, I have to go potty. I laughed.

I went to the restroom and let the liquid that needed to be let out.

I exited the restroom and was startled as something flew by and hit the wall. My phone was destroyed as I turned to look at the floor. I fought hard for this phone.

You fucked knew and didn't let me know! He yelled.

He discovered that I was aware.

Kelvin, I'm sorry, but I don't want to damage your relationship. I was interrupted by him.

"SIT DOWN, YOU TRAITOR FAG! YOU ARE BETTER THAN SHE!" He spoke.

My face was weeping while I was crying. Did he refer to me as gay?

Fortunately, your parents passed away so they wouldn't have to see a gay who is also a traitor. He spoke.

Sorry, I'm sorry. I said and bolted.

Kelvin's point of view

SHIT! How come I said that? This time, I knew I had crossed the boundary. In a little argument we once had, I insulted him. But this time, I went too far.

He finds talking about his parents to be challenging.

I then sprinted out of the home. When I spotted him, I ran after him.

I heard a smash and the sound of wheels squealing.

Oh no.

Chapter 5

Frank's point of view

I opened my eyes gradually. It shifted a little as it got used to the strong white light. Sitting up, I took a glance around.

Nature's splendor is all around me.

Green, tall grass was swaying in the breeze. Slowly, the flowers began to blossom. Bees buzzing, butterflies flitting, and birds singing. Both of my parents grinned.

My parents, what?

Frank, hello," my mother remarked.

I burst into tears and hurried to give them hugs. They are here? I can't believe it.

Wait, where exactly am I?

'Mom, Dad, I truly missed you,' I said. I said.

We also do. My dad said. However, you cannot remain here. he added.

"My beloved Frank, your time has not yet come. Heaven is where you are." mother said "Kelvin is expecting you. Close your eyes right now." she added.

When I closed my eyes, I faintly heard both of them say, "I love you."

I cautiously opened my eyes, and the harsh light irritated my eyes. Kelvin was sound asleep as I turned to look. He was holding my hand, I saw. I moved my fingers to gently shake him awake.

He started to gently wake up after I did that and gave me a look. But as soon as he turned to face me, I was overcome with flashbacks of our altercation, and my heart burst into a million pieces.

After what he said that evening, I was saddened. I then did the most idiotic thing imaginable to try to conceal my pain.

Identify yourself. I said.

He giggled apprehensively. "Are you kidding me, right?" He spoke.

"No. So who are you?" I spoke in a monotone. I made an effort to project a chilly mood.

He just gave me a surprised expression.

I must dial the doctor, I must. He made a stuttering exit from the room.

I let out a breath that I had been holding for a long time.

uneasy quiet for five minutes...

Following Kelvin, the doctor entered the room.

"Well, Mr. Maxwell, it's good to meet you. I'm delighted you're doing well now." The physician stated.

Oh, is that my name, then? I inquired while acting as if I was unsure of my name.

Yes, he replied.

The doctor checked on me for a few minutes and asked me some questions, to which I responded as an amnesiac would. advantages of being a geek. *wink*

He then left the room, leaving Kelvin and me in an uneasy stillness. I grinned as I glanced at him. He pretended to cough before he spoke.

So I'll introduce myself because you have amnesia. He spoke. "Kelvin Macsen, I'm your closest buddy. We have been friends since we were in diapers." He laughed.

"Really?!" I tried to seem amused as I said. I grinned as he nodded.

I have this sensation in my belly that makes my stomach growl. I believe I have read it before.

Oh, yes.

Guilt

I was mistaken when I assumed it was hunger. It was a shame. lying is wrong.

But I'll lie to my best buddy if doing so would enable me to move on and stop interfering in his life.

I'll do it for myself. For his future, I'll do anything. He wounded him once before, and I don't want it to happen again.

It's the best.

"I nearly forgot, it's your birthday tomorrow."

What, oh what? It's my birthday! I've been unconscious for two months. SHIT!

I tried my hardest to hide my disbelief as I answered, "Oh."

"So..." he said. Since it's your birthday tomorrow, would you please, he continued.

His comments caused my heart to beat quickly, which forced me to answer yes.

How am I expected to go from here?

Bless this heartless body.

Frank's point of view

"So..." he said. Since it's your birthday tomorrow, would you, well, please, he asked.

"What?" I said incoherently.

"Will you join me for a hangout tomorrow?" He queried. I just grinned and nodded in response.

Eeeeehhhh!!! OMG! Okay, go ahead and relax. This hangout is more than simply a "hangout," so don't label me as insane.

He implies a friendly date when he invites me to "hang out" without his pals.

For me, it's a date as couples go on dates, but it's simply a friendly date for him. Okay, presuming too much. gloomy life

Regardless, the door sprang open, and his companions entered. They also brought a cake, some balloons, and some flowers.

What's your state of mind? Darby enquired.

"Who are you, I-Uhh?" I replied anxiously. It was quite close.

Guys, he has amnesia. stated Kelvin. He also went through my results with everyone, which was a lie given that I had feigned amnesia.

Well, I'm Darby if that's the case. Darby extended his hand for a handshake. I can't help but notice the skepticism on his face, however, for some reason. I'm hoping he won't realize it.

I just smiled and shook his hand. For the last five minutes, everyone has been doing that.

A weird hand extended to shake mine. I turned to face the owner of the hand. A girl was there.

"Uhm... hey. Kelvin's girlfriend Nina here." She spoke.

Girlfriend? A new woman? That caused my heart to burst when the hammer struck it or was that simply the sound of a glass breaking? I'm not sure anymore. My heart was beating so hard it seemed like it was trying to escape from my ribs.

I was unaware that you had a girlfriend. I said. What a dreadful thing to say, you moron. Because of your "amnesia," it stands to reason that you are unaware of his girlfriend.

I only shook her hand and put on a phony grin to cover up my foolishness.

The world became quiet. Everyone was aware of my passion for my best buddy. except for him and his new partner.

They sensed the uncomfortable quiet. I just extended my arms and pretended to yawn.

"I'm drained. I want to snooze, "I stated.

Everyone said alright and they departed. everything except Kelvin. He remained. I just turned away from him and draped the blanket over my face.

I sobbed quietly while letting all of my tears fall. He shouldn't be aware that I'm sobbing, please. Oh my God, I'm so pitiful.

Why do I always get duped by him? Why did I ever fall for a straight man? My best buddy, not just any man.

Because only idiots fall in love with someone who won't return their affection.

My eyes were thick while I was weeping. I allow them to hold me and lead me into the realm of dreams.

Chapter 6

Frank's point of view

Thank God, I've been out of that dull hospital for a while. I've been standing outside Kelvin's room for maybe an hour now. Even if it's already 9:00 when he said to meet him at his home at 8 o'clock. The eighth time I knocked on his door, there was still no answer.

"Kelvin!!!" I yelled. If you do not, The door opening caused me to be interrupted.

"Within the restroom is Kelvin. What would you like?" Oh, Nina is here.

She is just wearing her underpants and a long sleeve top. Her hair is also unkempt.

"Uhh... I'm s-sorry if I d-disturbed you from what you were doing." I hesitated.

"It's okay. We just got done." She spoke.

Moments later, we were joined by a shirtless Kelvin.

"Hello, Frank! Birthday greetings!" He said with joy. "Are you up for an adventure?" he added. I just grinned at him. A grin to mask the heartache I've been experiencing.

I'll simply wait for you to get ready, I guess. I replied and walked over to the sofa in the living room.

I moaned. I'll thus celebrate my birthday this year in this manner. Be depressed, wounded, and heartbroken. Maybe in the future, this is how I'll celebrate my birthday.

Later, I saw Nina and Kelvin holding hands. While gazing at one another and kissing, they are grinning broadly. Seeing someone you love not be able to return the love was heartbreaking.

Are you prepared to leave? Kelvin questioned me. I just nod in response. Speaking will just lead me to stammer and weep, therefore I don't want to do it anymore.

We left the home and climbed into his vehicle. I was in the backseat and his girlfriend was in the front. I just turned aside from the scene in front of me.

We arrived at our location after 30 minutes. Our favorite location was there. Where you can still see our old tree home is in the forest.

"Our treehouse is here. We once gathered here." He spoke.

I believe I was mistaken in thinking he was talking to me. His girlfriend was the target of his remarks. Just grinning and kissing him, Nina.

I appreciate you bringing me here. She spoke.

I'm going to wander about, Kelvin. And on your date, keep to yourself.

"Okay." He spoke without turning to face me.

I just left the area and left the jungle. As I turned to look, I saw a cab. I motioned with my hand for the driver to halt. I entered the cab once it had stopped and drove home. I'll simply go home and have a little birthday celebration.

My tears started to run down my face. I regret having been born. I'm simply an error. I caused my parents to pass away. I was supposed to live alone. My dearest buddy gave me evidence of it.

As the automobile came to a halt, my tears didn't stop. I stepped outside and sprinted inside.

"SURPRISE!!!" Everyone's yells were audible.

I glanced at them before rushing to my room. I sat down on my bed and closed myself in my room. I sobbed while burying myself in my blanket.

Please open the door, Frank. Darby spoke, as I heard.

I said, "Leave me alone."

I sobbed non stop till I slept off.

TIME SKIP

When I opened my eyes, everyone was in my room.

"Congratulations, Frank!" While holding a cake, Darby spoke.

"How did you enter this place?" I muttered while turning my head away.

He replied, "Kelvin allowed us in." I saw Kelvin sitting on the bed.

"What?" I said coldly.

He apologized, he said.

"Let the two of you converse for a minute," I said. As everyone left the room, Darby remarked. My bed is where they left their presents.

I simply ignored him and went up.

Kelvin's point of view

He got out of bed, entered the bathroom, and shut the door. I knocked but got no answer.

Are you OK, I inquired.

"I am f-fine. Just p-please l-leave me alone." He is crying, and I can hear it.

I had a heaviness in my chest after hearing him say it. It has the sensation of being constantly poked with needles.

"Okay. I'll return later." I murmured and spoke gently.

I exited his home and began to go forward. I began remembering our early years while I was walking.

At the playground behind our school, I was having fun in the sandbox. Tip over the plastic buckets after filling them with sand. I tried to make a sand castle, but it kept falling apart.

Can we play together? the child stated.

"No," I remarked as I carried on trying to construct a sand castle. Thought the child had departed, but I noticed him take one of my buckets and add sand to it as well. I grabbed it from him out of rage. I could hear him sobbing, but I simply kept repeating the sandcastle-building procedure.

Some of the sand was blown away by the high wind. My right eye is stinging for me.

"MOMMY! SAND WAS IN MY EYE." I yelled, rubbing my palm over it.

"Slowly open your eyes. I'll extinguish it." I opened it gingerly even though it wasn't my mother's voice. I quickly blinked after sensing a breeze blowing my eye. The searing sensation quickly subsided. After a little adjustment, I was able to see the child.

Is your eye now alright? I nod as he asks.

"I'm grateful," I said. "Can you assist me in building a sand castle?" Since he assisted me with the sand in the eye issue, I requested him.

I handed him a bucket after he nodded. We rejoiced as we finished building our sandcastles after a short while.

With that remembrance, I grinned to myself. That day, I was absent.

When I arrived at my home, Nina was standing outside.

Hello, baby. She said and kissed me.

Hello, I said. Why are you at this location? Added I

I arrived to visit you. She spoke.

So, we went inside my bedroom and sat. I didn't listen as she began talking about things.

I'm sorry, but I don't get this. I muttered, frustratedly rubbing my skull. Despite reading the whole mathematical problem many times, I still don't know how to answer it.

I hear Frank giggling. He had already finished the task at hand. He is now resting on my bed, playing a game on his phone.

You want aid, he inquired.

I said, "Yes, please."

He then read the issue from the book and guided me through the solution.

I presented it to him a short while later to check if it was accurate. He handed it to me and nodded in agreement.

"Kelvin!" Nina called name. Are you alright? she asked.

"Yes, I'm doing OK. I merely thought about my early times with Frank." I said while grinning.

"Say his name once again." She spoke.

"Frank." I then grinned.

Why did you go out with me? It was her.

"I like you, so. Nina, you're stunning." I said.

"You're so foolish, damn it. Yes, you like me, but Frank is your true love." She spoke.

I said incredulously, "What?"

"Say his name once again." She spoke.

Her fingers halted me mid-"Chr-"

"See. You are grinning. Just tell him before it's too late that you adore him. I'll be OK." She spoke.

I questioned, "I love him?".

"Yes. If you didn't love him, you wouldn't be so concerned about him. If you didn't love him, you wouldn't think about him." She spoke. "I can also see it in Kelvin's eyes. More than simply a buddy, he loves you." she added.

Perhaps she is correct. No, disregard it. She is accurate.

I then sprinted back to his place. I kept running and running. When I got there, I walked directly to his bedroom. I opened it, but nothing was inside.

"Frank!" I yelled. He wasn't anywhere to be found when I went looking for him around the home.

I saw something as I entered the kitchen. The white paper was nicely folded.

To my dearest buddy, Kelvin, I adored it read.

I read it after I opened it.

Kelvin, hello. I just wanted to express my gratitude for everything. For our wonderful friendship's many years. I've never had a better friend than you, yet I'm simply a burden to you. I apologize.

I apologize for making up for my amnesia. I could never forget you. I had a flawless memory of everything. I'm such a moron, right?

I cherish you. You're not simply a buddy; you're my lover. I'm a coward for telling you about it in this letter, I freely acknowledge. I adore you and want the best for you. Love the person who brings you joy and makes your heart race. Isn't that what love is? Even if I'm not the cause of your happiness, it makes me glad to see you happy.

I purposely withheld my departure from you since I didn't want to continue to annoy you with my drama.

Have I expressed my affection for you? Oh, yes.

I'll say goodbye and I love you.

Sincerely yours, Frank.

Tears started to stream down my cheeks as I finished reading the letter. It's too late now.

I'm such a moron.

Chapter 7

Kelvin's Point of view

After a few years...

"Daddy, goodbye. I cherish you." Amelia kissed me and said. She then dashed inside her classroom.

I sighed.

Within the last several years, things have altered. My despair worsened after he departed. I became engaged in a gang and got into a lot of fights. I got into a lot of difficulties because of it, which led to my expulsion. I thus never get to complete high school.

My biological daughter Amelia was conceived as a consequence of having unprotected intercourse with a party girl. She wanted to get an abortion when she found out she was pregnant. But I declined. I assured her that I would look after the child once she was born.

Her mother passed away before Amelia was born. While the woman was giving delivery, there were issues.

I now just have Amelia left. My family abandoned me as a result of what I did. I thus asked Darby if we might remain at their home while I looked for work and a place to rent. I'm hoping he concurred.

I managed to find a job and a place to live, so we remained there for a year.

I'm currently employed at a café. serving consumers after asking for their orders. The café's elderly proprietor was exceedingly kind. She also provided us with lodging. Even if life is still difficult, I can get by.

I'm on my way back to the café right now. I've never been able to afford a vehicle. I passed the dance school Amelia wanted to attend while I was walking. Every time we travel home, she always stops and checks out the school's name. However, I never had the funds to cover the cost.

I wish I could grant her every request. Let her go through what other young females go through. like ballet, or visit the mall and get a brand-new set of toys and other enjoyable items. But I'm not wealthy.

As I walked inside the café, the bell rang. My nose was assaulted by the aroma of freshly baked goodies, and I could hear people conversing as usual.

I changed into my outfit and began serving the public. I smile at the folks I'm serving. They also smiled and gave me their order.

The bell rang to announce the entrance of a client. I proceeded to the table where he had chosen to sit as a result.

Izzy's Café welcomes you; how may I assist you? I remarked, drawing the man's attention.

"Oh, wait, is that Kelvin? Are you there?" A guy spoke.

I looked at him in perplexity.

"My name is Darby. Man, I miss you." It's Darby, I see. He had a new appearance. He seemed like an adult.

"Hey, dude. What's up?" I said.

"I'm good. Who are you? How's your daughter doing?" He spoke.

"We're good. Life is still difficult, but I can get by." I answered.

After a time, we caught up on everything that had transpired. He disclosed to me his occupation as an architect. He displayed images of his sketches to me. a sketch of a home, a bridge, and a building.

"Frank is indeed back. At the mall yesterday, I ran into him." He spoke.

His name made my heart beat more quickly than usual. He's back?

I questioned, "When did he come back?"

"Last week. He informed me that he was here on business." He spoke.

Business?

Darby looked at the time.

"I apologize, but I must go. I'm going to meet someone. We'll discuss this more later." He spoke. Call me if you need anything while I'm here. He handed me his number before leaving.

I kept working after that until I had to go fetch Amelia. I, therefore, took a stroll to the school. Amelia was on the swing when I got there. She seemed dejected.

Hello, Mr. Macsen. May I speak with you? Teacher enquired.

"You may, indeed. Ma'am, what is it?" I enquired in fear.

"During their break, your daughter escaped. For one hour, she was gone. We made every effort to locate her, but we were unable." She spoke. "The fact that a guy brought her back is fortunate. You need to speak to your daughter about her actions." I only nodded. "And here, one more item." I got a document from her. A list of textbooks is provided.

I then headed over to Amelia.

Hello there, young lady. I said while grinning. She regrettably raised her head.

"Dad, I'm sorry." She spoke.

"All right, sweetie. I'm glad you're fine." I said. Let's go out and get these books now. Added I

So we headed to the neighborhood book shop. I had a look at the list and then I went in search of the books. I proceeded to the cashier to purchase the books.

It would cost $500. A guy spoke.

I examined my wallet. It is just $100.

Can I pay for it tomorrow, please? I queried.

No, he replied.

"Please? I lack the necessary funds. My daughter also needs it." I said.

Before I summon the guards, leave. He spoke.

"Come on, Amelia. I remarked while sighing. The worst father ever is me. Sorry Amelia, I was unable to purchase your books. Added I

"You're OK, Daddy. Still, I adore you." I added, "I love you, too," in response to what she said.

We then exited the shop and began to stroll.

But I was forced to stop when my shoulder was touched.

You left them, sir. A guy spoke.

My whole world came to a halt as I turned to face him.

Kelvin's point of view

"Kelvin?" He remarked while grinning. Good or bad? He queried.

"I, I'm alright," I stumbled as I said.

Once again, hello, Amelia. He smiled.

She said, "Hello Mr. Prince."

"You two are acquainted?" I queried. I said, "And why did she call you Mr. Prince?"

"Yeah. I noticed her when I was walking to my lesson from the dance studio." He answered. "because I am Swan Lake's Prince. That is the reason." He added while grinning.

So, how are you doing? I queried.

I'm all right. He answered. Oh yes, how clumsy am I? He continued and dug into his pocket for something. "Tomorrow I'm getting married here. You ought to go. Bring Amelia along."

He said goodbye and then glanced at his watch.

Goodbye...

Hello, Frank...

Frank, my dearest buddy, bye.

I'm leaving the guy I found love with...

He's abandoning me once again. This time, he said his goodbyes before leaving. a farewell that isn't expressed in a note or letter.

Let's go home, Daddy. Added Amrlia.

I'm good, baby. I answered, flashing her a dejected grin.

Chapter 8

Kelvin's point of view

"Daddy, where are we going?" Amelia enquired.

We're attending Mr. Prince's wedding, she said. I responded, brushing away my tears.

A time back, a parcel that claimed to be from Frank showed up. Both the outfit and the dress were white. I assumed it to be the wedding's theme. White. We're now traveling to the church.

We arrived at the wedding location a little while later. People were all sitting and conversing.

"Excuse me, Frank, where are you?" I turned to a stranger.

He is in the changing area. He responded, and I thanked him.

Amelia and I then entered the changing room. I saw him wearing an identical white suit when we arrived.

He said, "Hey, kel-." But I interrupted him by embracing him. He hugged me, and I could feel it.

Frank, I know it's too late for me to say I love you. I said as tears flowed freely down my cheeks.

He let go of the embrace and fixed his eyes on mine.

It's OK, As he kissed my forehead, he murmured.

TIME SKIP

Everyone got to their feet as the wedding march began to play and the door opened. Frank grinned broadly as he proceeded down the aisle.

He was staring straight at me. I grinned, "I know my heart is fairly broken. Despite how agonizing it was to see him go down the aisle toward the man he was meant to marry, I smiled.

I noted that there was no groom there when Frank got close to the altar.

Excuse me, but I was wondering where the groom was. I inquired of the man who sat next to me.

He just grinned without responding to the query.

Could you kindly ask Kelvin Macsen to come up front? Frank's voice is audible.

Despite my confusion, I walked up to the altar.

I simply stared at him bewildered until I saw him grin. What is going on?

I approached him and he grasped my hand.

"I apologize to Kelvin Macsen, my dearest and greatest friend. I'm sorry I made you feel bad. I came here to do two vital tasks. One is to express regret. Two more "He got on one knee and bowed. is to inquire of you.

'Will you wed me?' He queried.

What?

My eyes are turning like a waterfall, and my heart is going to burst.

"Y-yes. You will be my wife." I replied as I hugged him. Never leave me again, please. I cried and said,

"I swear. I cherish you, Kelvin. I've loved you more than a buddy ever since we were little." He spoke.

I then gave him a passionate kiss while gazing into his eyes.

Ultimately, my best buddy and I were hitched. Amelia was overjoyed to learn that he would visit Mr. Prince every day. I get to see my closest friend who also happens to be my hubby every day.

Even though there may be many challenges in life, a rainbow will eventually appear.

THE END

www.ingramcontent.com/pod-product-compliance
Lightning Source LLC
LaVergne TN
LVHW050332160826
845677LV00014B/3603

* 9 7 9 8 3 5 1 7 5 2 8 0 8 *